Why I Waited
A Guide to Maintaining Your Virginity

Angela R. Camon

Edited By

Carl L. Camon
Andrea Story

Note for Librarians: A cataloguing record for this book is available from Library
and Archives Canada at www.collectionscanada.ca/amicus/index-e.html

Printed in Victoria, BC, Canada.

ISBN: 978-1-4269-0038-9 (sc)

ISBN: 978-1-4269-0040-2 (e-book)

*We at Trafford believe that it is the responsibility of us all, as both individuals and corporations,
to make choices that are environmentally and socially sound. You, in turn, are supporting this
responsible conduct each time you purchase a Trafford book, or make use of our publishing
services.*
To find out how you are helping, please visit www.trafford.com/responsiblepublishing.html

*Our mission is to efficiently provide the world's finest, most comprehensive book publishing
service, enabling every author to experience success. To find out how to publish your book, your
way, and have it available worldwide, visit us online at www.trafford.com*

Trafford rev. 8/19/2009

 www.trafford.com

North America & international
toll-free: 1 888 232 4444 (USA & Canada)
phone: 250 383 6864 ♦ fax: 250 383 6804 ♦ email: info@trafford.com

The United Kingdom & Europe
phone: +44 (0)1865 487 395 ♦ local rate: 0845 230 9601
facsimile: +44 (0)1865 481 507 ♦ email: info.uk@trafford.com

Dedication

I dedicate this book to all the young people across this great nation and abroad who have displayed the courage to abstain from sex until marriage. I commend you and hope that you always remember you are worth the wait! I dedicate this book to those who have indulged in the lifestyle of sexual promiscuity. You can be renewed! Whatever point you are in life, whether you are living a life of respect in the highest regard or whether you have made a litany of mistakes, thank you for allowing me to pour into your lives. Please know that God loves you. You are fearfully and wonderfully made. You have what it takes to weather any storm, to fight any temptation and win any battle because you are more than a conqueror! You are an over comer!

Regardless of your race, socioeconomic status, demographical location, you are someone important in the eyesight of God. You are unique in your own right! Many have said you are a lost generation, but I disagree, you are not lost, and you are traveling on the road that leads to a bright future. You are destined to become something great. You can do all things through Christ, which strengthens you *(Philippians 4:13)*. I come against every negative word that has ever been spoken to you or about you. I come against every generational curse in the powerful and matchless name of Jesus Christ. The yoke of generational curses stops with you. You are covered in the blood of Jesus!

You are above and not beneath. You are the head and not the tail. Jesus said that he came that you might have life and have it more abundantly *(John 10:10)*. I decree and declare that you have life and live in abundance. I decree that you will not be enticed by the schemes and ploys that Satan has orchestrated for your ruin. I decree that you will not be lured into the world of negativity that will inevitably contaminate your mind, but that you will embrace life with an optimistic viewpoint. I declare that every vision that God has put into your spirit will come to pass. *For the vision is yet for an appointed time, but at the end it shall speak, and not lie: though it tarry, wait for it: because it will surely come, it will not tarry (Habakkuk 2:3).* I challenge each of you to discover your talents, maximize your full potential, reach for the stars, dare to be a dreamer, and walk in your destiny!

Acknowledgements

I give all glory, praise, and honor to my Lord and Savior Jesus Christ. I thank you for the strength that you gave to me to wait. Thank you for the inspiration to write this book. To my husband, Carl, thank you for your love, support and encouragement, you were definitely worth the wait. To my four miracles - Carl Jr., Aaron, Camille, and Candace: I love you all forever. To my parents Dr. Vickery and the late Pauline Williams, thank you for teaching me the Word of God and for being a living example. To my sisters Tracie, Vickie, and Kyna, you all are truly an inspiration to me. Thank you for your prayers. To my pastor, Pastor Madine Camon, all I can say is "But God". Thank you for your support and encouragement.

Introduction

Sex, Sex, Sex! The topic of sex is being discussed and debated all over the world. Whether it is the latest gossip among teenage friends or on a national level, where our leaders are considering the possibility of legalizing gay marriages, sex is a very prominent idea and topic. Members of our society are bombarded with commercials on television advertising products that claim to increase your sexual pleasure. Movies are filled with men and women engaging in enticing hot sex scenes. Chat rooms, instant messaging programs and websites have opened the window of opportunity for everyone to indulge him or herself in the world of sex. Society has attempted to lure us into thinking that sex is a "plaything" or an ordinary experience that equates to a spring break fling or a one-night stand. Viewing women and men as sex symbols, Hollywood sets the stage for portraying a false illusion of what true love really is.

It's no wonder you have sex on your mind, it's all around you. Sex is a topic that you can't avoid. Since you will be confronted with issues concerning sex, it is important that you are as knowledgeable as possible. Knowledge is power. Contrary to what some of you may have been taught or what you have heard from your friends, sex is not a dirty word. However, in many cases it has been abused and misused for reasons other than for what God created it. There are many perceptions about what sex is all about. Regardless of what your perception of sex is, the only viewpoint that really matters is God's. I hope that this book will give you a new perspective, even if you think that you have heard it all or think you know all there is to know about sex. It is not my intent to insult your intelligence or the beliefs of those who may have a strong grasp about what sex is all about. I challenge you to read this book from cover to cover and to discover some new information that you can add to your bank of knowledge. My sole purpose in writing this book is to encourage you to wait until you are married to have sex. I am a living witness that you can abstain from sex until you are married, if you truly want too. It is not only my intent to offer you encouragement to wait to have sex, but I also want to give you reasons why you should wait based on the Word of God. It is not enough just to encourage you to wait, but you also need to know why you are waiting. Whoever you are and whatever your past experiences may have been, it is my prayer that by sharing my personal experiences about some of the circumstances that I encountered, you may be helped in some way. Learning what God says about sex and learning how it can affect your life will hopefully encourage you to appreciate sex for what it is worth. It is my prayer that you will be encouraged to make a personal commitment to wait until you are married. I also want to offer a word of encouragement to those who have already had a sexual encounter. It is not too late for you. You can be restored. So regardless of where you are in your life, my goal is to help you discover God's truth, so your vision is not clouded by the lies of the enemy.

Table of Contents

Chapter 1

Why I Waited

B efore I share my insight about why I waited to have sex until I was married, let me begin by saying that I understand exactly how you feel. I know how it feels to have your hormones raging. I am in tune with the emotional highs and lows of the teenage years. Believe it or not, I too was once a teenager. I can identify with the pressure that comes with being a teenager. With some guidance and prayer you can get through this period in your life.

I was blessed with a lot of influential people in my life. My parents were very instrumental in helping me to reach the decision to wait until I was married to have sex. My mother would talk to my sister Tracie and I, and would emphasize the importance of us having self-respect. She said, "you can't expect anyone to respect you, if you don't respect yourself, and if you lay down with those boys, they won't even have respect for you the next morning." My mom was extremely to the point. She made it very clear that she didn't want us to have sex until we were married. Although it wasn't funny then, I now find it hilarious when I think about some of the scare tactics that she used. The most memorable one is her telling me that the pain of childbirth was like a watermelon coming through your nose. It sounds comical, and perhaps a little bizarre, but it sure did work. It also helped knowing that my mom was a virgin when she got married. I had the kind of mom who led by example. I was truly blessed.

Ultimately my dad was on the same wavelength as my mom, except he was a little firmer than she was. My dad just came to the point and said, "You are not going to bring any babies in this house." He didn't give me any options. He was such an authority figure that when he spoke everybody listened and took him at his word. If he said I wasn't bringing any babies in that house, then you better believe I wasn't going to bring any babies in that house.

I was blessed to be raised in a Christian home, with parents who taught me according to the Word of God. They taught me that God would not be pleased with me having sex before marriage. I didn't want to let my parents down and most certainly did not want to let God down.

Another influential person in my life was Mrs. Fannie Corbin, who was the youth coordinator at Springfield Missionary Baptist Church, in Warner Robins, Georgia. I was a member of a teen group called the Red Circle. We met on Wednesday and we discussed several issues that teenagers were facing at that time. One particular issue was sex. It seemed that no matter what other topic that we discussed, we always talked about sex. One key point that Mrs. Corbin taught me was that I was worth waiting for. She said that no matter how handsome and smart a guy is, I shouldn't let him pressure me into doing something that I was not ready to do. She taught me not to be influenced by the things that he could do for me like buying me clothes, giving me money, or getting me a new hairdo, because I am worth the wait. If he truly loves me, he will wait.

It is no secret that all of my aunts were dear to me in their own right, but my mom's sister, Aunt Helen as I called her, was very special to me. My friends and some of my family would often wonder why I would visit Aunt Helen as much as I did. I was practically at her house almost everyday. I spent so much time with her and her four children that it seemed like I was apart of their family. In ways that Aunt Helen didn't even realize, she was very instrumental in helping me keep my virginity. She would encourage me in ways that had a lasting effect. She would never come right out and say, "don't have sex," but she would make a comment like "keep yourself up." She didn't need to say anything else, because I always knew what she meant.

I have a certain respect for all of my sisters for various reasons, but I have a deep respect for my sister Tracie. She has always been a leader and has set a good example for my younger sisters and me. I don't think I ever told her, but she was very influential in some of the decisions that I made in my life, including abstaining from sex. I knew that my big sister had carried herself with much dignity and self-respect, and I wanted to follow in her footsteps. She waited to have sex until she got married, and so I planned to do the same. I can remember when she got married; she made life seem so glamorous.

While I will admit I don't remember all of my teachers, there is one teacher who I will always remember, Mrs. Diane Moore. Mrs. Moore was my high school English teacher at Northside High School in Warner Robins, Georgia. Not only did she teach me about reading comprehension, mechanics of grammar, and how to write an essay, but she also taught me about life. She taught me to set goals for myself and to never stop until I had achieved them. Mrs. Moore had high expectations for all of her students, and she didn't mind letting us know it. We didn't have much of a choice; we were all expected to do well, with no exceptions. It seemed that she always had a word of encouragement, especially when things were not going so well.

It has been over twenty years since I was in Mrs. Moore's class, but I still remember some of the encouraging words that she gave me. She would tell me "Angie, you have great potential to be any thing that you want to be in life." I will admit at first I didn't believe what she was saying, but she said it with such confidence that eventually I started believing it myself. I had such great respect for Mrs. Moore back then and still do today. I didn't want to do anything to cause her to be disappointed in me. I often reflect on some of the things that I learned in her class, some of which were instrumental in shaping my life today.

Finally, I hold in dearest regard my grandmother, Mrs. Jeanie Mae Foster. In addition to my parents and others my grandmother was my role model. Because of her strong faith in God and her wisdom, she inspired me to become all that I could be. Often times she would encourage me with a simple but yet profound phrase such as "Just trust God." This phrase was, to my grandmother, the answer for all of life's problems. I can remember on more than one occasion she would tell me that she loved me and that if I kept being a "good girl," as she referred to it, then God would bless me and give me a good husband one day.

My parents laid the foundation, but God had so many other people to build on that foundation. It is because of the people in my life that I was dedicated to making a vow and making a commitment to keep it.

Factors That Influence Me to Wait

Although it has been over 20 years since I was teenager, I can still remember some of the phrases that the boys used back then. The most common one was "If you love me you will have sex with me." Others were "I have needs and if you are my girl you are suppose to take care of my needs," and "If we have sex, our relationship will be closer." They even made promises that they would be careful so that I wouldn't get pregnant. Some of the boys would try to charm themselves into my life by telling me how pretty I looked or how smart I was. I can't say that some of the lines that the boys used were not flattering, but there were too many other factors that quickly helped me to get over being flattered. Unfortunately, I had plenty examples of how girls were being used for sex. You know the game. The boy tells the girl how pretty and fine she is, and he convinces her that he loves her and only her. Then he eventually talks her into having sex, only to find out later that she was not the only girl that he has been having sex with. The next day he gets with his friends and talk about the sexual experience that they had together. In some cases, after having sex the boy wouldn't even talk to the girl. He didn't want anything else to do with her. I knew that I didn't want to experience rejection of that magnitude.

I have also seen sex in teen relationships viewed from a different perspective. I once had a friend who was in what turned out to be an unhealthy relationship. In the beginning, everything was okay in their relationship, at least until they started having sex. Once they started having sex, he became very jealous. He felt like she belonged to him, as if she was his property. He didn't like for her to talk to anyone else. I will never forget one day after school she and I were talking and two boys came up and simply spoke to us. It made my friend's boyfriend angry, so he beat her. I tried to explain to her that she didn't deserve that kind of treatment, and she should get out of the relationship, but she felt trapped. She stayed in the relationship and endured numerous beatings because of her boyfriend's jealous rages. I knew that was not the life for me.

I had a friend in high school that I will never forget. We were the best of friends and we often talked about life and how we wanted to get married one day. We had already decided what kind of husbands we were going to have, what kind of houses we would live in, what kind of cars we would drive, and how many kids we would have. As friends, we made a pact that we would never have sex until we were married. For many years, we held on to that pact. From time to time, we would ask each other "Are you still holding on?" What we were really asking each other was "Are you still a virgin?" Usually, we would each reply, "Yeap, I'm still holding on." But one day, when we were doing our "virginity check," which is what I liked to call it, she asked me "Are you still holding on?" I gave my usual reply, which was yes, but this time when I asked her she didn't say anything. So I asked her again, hoping that maybe she didn't hear me. She had indeed heard me, but didn't respond because she didn't know how to tell me that she had broken our pact. She had sex with her boyfriend in the backseat of his car.

I was not only hurt because she broke the pact between us, but I was also hurt because of the pain she felt. She had sacrificed the precious gift of her virginity only to find out later that her boyfriend was not as in love with her as he had proclaimed. Months later, after their first sexual experience, my friend found out that the only reason that her boyfriend wanted to have to sex with her was so that he could cause her to break her pact. He saw her losing her virginity as a game. Once he got her hooked and they had sex, he moved on to the next girl. This left my friend emotionally distraught. Not only was she carrying the emotional baggage from the guilt of having sex in the first place, but now she had to deal with the shame of being manipulated by her boyfriend. My friend was in such an emotional state that she tried to kill herself. Thank God she was not successful in her actions and she was able to go to counseling to get the help that she needed. Having sex had a negative impact on my friend's life.

Among the factors of having influential people in my life, and the experiences that I saw my friends go through, I think that the most significant reason that I decided to remain abstinent until I was married was because of my love for God. I was saved at the age of 13. I didn't understand everything there was to know about God, but I knew that he loved me and I loved him. As I look back over my life, I realize now that I had a special anointing. God had set me apart from my friends, so that I wouldn't get involved in some of the things that they were involved in, because of this special anointing. This was not to say that I didn't want to have sex, but even if I did want to, the Holy Spirit would not let me. Even at an early age, I knew that God had a divine purpose for my life and I didn't want to taint God's plan.

The older I got and the more I studied the Bible, I realized how important it was to please God. I learned that my body was God's temple and I didn't have the right to defile it. I was saved at the age of 13, but it was at the age of 14 that I dedicated my body to the Lord. Dedicating my body to the Lord was a lot easier to say than to do. It was difficult to not have sex, especially when all of my friends were talking about the good times they were having (or they thought they were having). It was difficult to fight the urge to want to have sex, but I continued to fight because I knew that there would be consequences to my actions, and those were consequences that I didn't want to have to face. I prayed and asked God to help me. The desire to have sex was strong, but I continued to pray. The word of God and the advice of the influential people in my life helped me refrain from having sex.

It was because of my decision to wait to have sex that I didn't have many boyfriends. Oh sure I had friends, but I never considered them to be my boyfriends. Most of the guys that I associated with could not handle being in a relationship with me without having sex. Since I was not willing to conform to their requests to meet their sexual needs, our relationships usually didn't last very long. When I told the guys that I was waiting until I was married to have sex, some of them were straightforward in telling me that they could not wait that long. Others would try to string me along telling me that they would wait, only to find out in the end that they actually were not waiting, but was having sex with someone else. The logic behind their undermining schemes was that they didn't want to lose a good thing (me), but they also wanted to have some fun (sex). I had some boys in my life that stayed around long enough to see if they could get me to change my mind, but to no avail. Regardless of the circumstances, I refused to let down my standards.

Oh yes, you better believe that I had standards! Having high standards is another reason why I didn't have many boyfriends. You see, I didn't just associate with anybody. I can't remember where I heard this saying, but it says, "If you lay down with dogs, you will get up with fleas." I lived by that motto. It took more than a guy telling me that I was pretty or fine to get my attention; he had to have something going for himself. I didn't have shallow standards like thinking that he had to be a certain height, weight or things of that nature, but I focused on more important issues such as does he go to church, is he doing well in school, and does he treat me with respect? I was more interested in his character than how well he could dress or the material things that he could give me.

Because of my standards, my friends and some of my family members would tell me that I would never get married. However, I didn't let that deter me, because I knew that if I held on to my standards God would bless me with the person that he had planned for me to have. I held on to my standards and I didn't back down. I was ridiculed and called all kinds of names. Many guys and girls accused me of being arrogant because of the way that I conducted myself. Despite of what others believed, I was not arrogant, but I did have class. I only associated with people who would build me up and not tear me down. I am sure that you have heard the phrase "If you don't stand for something, then you will fall for anything." I took that to heart. I made a commitment to live a life that was pleasing to God, holy and pure, because I didn't want to fall into the trap of living a life of sin. I didn't offer any apologies to my friends for the decision that I had made.

As time went on, I had grown tired of the games of little boys masquerading as men, yet lacking the stamina to make a faithful commitment to me. I decided to end all relationships and focus my attention on my relationship with Jesus. That was the best decision that I could have ever made. I would spend my time praying and reading the Word of God. A few of the scriptures that I read were Psalms 23, Philippians 4:13, Matthew 21:22, Jeremiah 29:11, and Ephesians 3:20. The more I read and spent time with Jesus, the stronger I became.

Strategies that I used to help me keep my commitment

Your spirit and flesh are in constant war with one another. The sinful nature desires what is contrary to the Spirit, and the Spirit desires what is contrary to the sinful nature. There is a constant battle warring over whether or not to give in to your flesh. The battle between your spirit and flesh can be compared to the game of tug-of- war. Tug-of-war is a contest in which two opposing teams tug on opposite ends of a rope, each trying to pull the other across a dividing line. It is a struggle for supremacy. Your spirit is on one end of the rope and your flesh is on the other end. Your flesh is pulling against your spirit and your spirit is pulling against your flesh. The stronger force will defeat the other side. That is why you have to prepare for the battle, so that your spirit can win. As with any battle, you must have a game plan if you expect to win. There were several strategies that I used to help me keep my commitment.

1. **Prayer -** Prayer was the most beneficial mechanism that I relied on most often. I knew that I couldn't fight this battle on my own, so I asked God for help. I would pray every morning and ask God to give me the strength to keep my vow. I would pray again at night to thank him for the strength that was given to me. Perhaps you will find it humorous, as some of my friends did, but before I went out on a date I would say a prayer. I prayed that God would help me to avoid getting into compromising situations. Keeping my vow was important to me. I made it one of my top priorities.

2. **Chose friends wisely -** I only associated with people who would respect me, and the decisions that I made for myself. I didn't make it a habit to associate with those who I knew would try to discourage me from keeping my vow. My friends didn't necessarily agree with everything that I believed, but they still offered me support for the decision that I made.

3. **Avoided temptations -** I would not be very truthful if I said that I have never been tempted, because I have. However, I did my very best not to put myself into compromising situations. I tried to double date with my friend as often as possible because it helped to have a friend to hold me accountable. There were times that I couldn't rely on double dating. During those times I tried to avoid the two of us being alone as much as

possible. We would go bowling or skating or any place where other people would be around.

4. **Guarded my mind** - I was very careful in choosing the kind of movies that I watched and the music that I listened too. I didn't watch movies that would entice me to emulate what was portrayed in the movies. I didn't listen to the type of music that would tempt me to act on the message that the lyrics of the songs were conveying.

5. **Communicated with positive adults -** The last thing that some teenagers want to do is to talk to adults, especially their parents. However, I found that talking to adults was very beneficial in helping me keep my virginity, and it helped in several other areas of my life as well I shared with you the influential people who I was blessed to have in my life. They were there to give me the godly advice that I needed. I couldn't imagine my life without them.

6. **Read the Word of God** - I shared with you earlier some of the scriptures that I read. Those scriptures, and so many others, were beneficial in every area of my life. Reading the Word of God gave me the strength that I needed. It gave me the assurance that God was on my side, and with him I could do all things. I realized that nothing was impossible if I continued to trust God.

7. **Developed a relationship with Jesus** - It was my mother who led me to Christ. She would always talk about God's love and how important it was to have Jesus as Lord and Savior. She would tell my sisters and I that we had to invite Jesus into our hearts for ourselves; she couldn't do it for us. Although she couldn't invite Jesus into our hearts for us, she lived a life that encouraged us to accept Jesus as our savior. She would encourage us to read the Word of God. I remember she would say, "You better learn to read the Word of God because you will need it one day." My mom had a lot of sayings, but one that I remember in particular was

her telling us to "Eat the Word of God." At that time, it was puzzling to me why my mom would be telling me to eat the bible, but now I realize that it was her way of telling me to mediate on the Word of God. She was, in essence, saying read the Word so much, until it becomes a part of you. Remember I told you earlier that I was saved at the age 13? Of course I didn't know everything there was to know about being saved, but I learned more as I continued to study the Word of God, attended church, and followed in the footsteps of the many people God placed in my life that were filled with wisdom. I had a love for God, and I didn't want to do anything to hinder my relationship with him. I knew that it wouldn't please God if I broke the commitment that I made.

Reflection

1. Think about the strategies that I used. What are some other strategies that you can use?

_____

_____

_____

_____

_____

_____

Chapter 2

Why You Should Wait

I have shared with you the influential people in my life and the factors that influenced me to wait until I was married to have sex. Now I want to talk about you. This section is not intended to lecture you, but rather to inform you about this powerful three-letter word **SEX!**

Perhaps you may be thinking to yourself, "It was my choice to wait until I was married, but what does that have to do with you?" You are absolutely right that waiting was my choice, and you have the right to make your own choice. I would like to offer some reasons why you should wait so that you can make an informed decision.

I think it is only proper to begin our discussion with what God says about sex. God has a lot to say; after all, he is the creator of sex. Everything that God created is beautiful, so I guess it is safe to say that sex is beautiful in God's eyesight. Laws have changed and society has become more accepting of sex outside of marriage, but God still has the same viewpoint. His view is the right view and it will never change. God's design for sex was created only for married couples. That's right! Only married people have the right to have sex. I know that you know some people who aren't married and yet they are sexually active. I know some too! It happens, but that is not God's way. God ordained sex for marriage.

Marriage is honorable and the bed undefiled, but fornicators and adulterers, God will judge (Hebrews 13:4). Those who are having sex outside of God's will (fornicators and adulterers), will be punished. Because God loves you so much, and he doesn't want to have to judge you, he gives clear instructions on how we are to conduct ourselves when it comes to sex. It is important to realize that your body does not belong to you, but it belongs to God. *I Corinthians 6:19 -20 says "What? Know ye not that your body is the temple of the Holy Ghost which is in you, which ye have of God, and ye are not your own? For ye are bought with a price; therefore glorify God in your body, and in your spirit, which are God's."*

Your body belongs to God! When you engage in immoral sexual acts like fornication, you bring disgrace to your body (God's temple). That is why God gives the warning to flee from fornication. Your body was not designed for fornication, but for God's purpose. *"Now the body is not for fornication, but for the Lord; and the Lord for the body" (I Corinthians 6:13).* It is so important that you take heed to God's warning and not follow the example of the 23,000 that died in one day because they committed fornication (*I Corinthians 10:8*).

God's Word clearly teaches us that he will judge those who don't obey his instructions concerning sex. God was serious about premarital sex (sex before marriage) in times past and he still is today. It was once a law that if a girl was charged with not being a virgin, she would be brought to the door of her father's house and the men of her town would stone her to death. Being promiscuous while living in her father's house was viewed as disgraceful (See Deuteronomy 22nd Chapter).

There are a number of reasons why you should wait until you are married to have sex, but the main reason that you should wait to have sex is because God said so. All other reasons come secondary to what God said. Although I think that addressing these three important topics: reputation, respect, and relationships, could categorize all of the reasons why you should wait. I will discuss other reasons as well. Let's start our discussion on why you should wait by addressing the three R's.

1. Reputation

Your character says a lot about you. If you are known to be "easy", then the boys will hang around you. I can remember this girl in one of my classes that seemed to be so popular. Actually, she was popular, but for the wrong reasons. All of the guys hung around her. She had black boys, white boys, fat boys, skinny boys, smart boys and not so smart boys hanging around her. They hung around her because they knew that she would have sex with anybody who wanted to have sex. It seemed like all the guys really liked her, and they led her to believe that they cared. Actually, that wasn't the case at all. Those guys were just hanging around for sex. Even though they had sex with her, they would talk about her and call her profane names in front of their friends. They were so disrespectful to her.

I remember hearing one of the guys tell his friend "I just have sex with her because I want to have fun and she'll do anything, but I don't really like her." I will never forget the look on this girl's face when she asked the guys if they would take her to a social dance at our school, and they all laughed. One guy said, "You actually think any of us want to be seen with you?" She was good enough to have sex with, but she wasn't good enough to take to a dance.

The clothes that you wear also have an affect on your reputation. Believe it or not, your clothes speak volumes about you. Clothes are the way that we package ourselves, they are how we show whom we are and what we think of ourselves. If you dress in clothes that emphasize your sexuality, you are sending the wrong message. The elderly generation were firm believers that young ladies were not suppose to show everything that God gave them, but they were suppose to dress appropriately. In many cases your good name and reputation is all that you have, so don't ruin it. *Proverbs 22:1 says, "A good name is rather to be chosen than great riches, and loving favor rather than silver and gold."*

2. Relationships

During your course of life you will be involved in many relationships. You will have a relationship with your parents, your friends, your teachers, and your church leaders, to name a few. Of all the relationships that you will ever take part in, your relationship with Jesus is the most important. *Jesus said that we are his friends if we follow his commandments (John 15:14).* If you do not follow his commandments you are not his friend. I don't know about you, but I don't want to do anything to hinder my relationship with Jesus. That is why I try my best to adhere to his commandments, so I can continue to be his friend.

I encourage you to do the same. Jesus wants to have a relationship with each of us, but he will not engage in a relationship with us, if we are living in sin. If we are not obedient to God and continue to practice sin, we can destroy our relationship with Jesus. God loves you. He created you for his glory. He wants you to be obedient to his word. He has commanded that we wait to have sex until we are married. If we choose to do it our way instead of God's way, then we will have to suffer the consequences. God will judge us. He cannot allow us to sin against our body that he created for his glory. God wants the best for us. He gave us commandments concerning sex to protect us. Having sex before you are married affects your relationship with Jesus in a profound way.

The following paragraphs tell the stories of two fictional characters whose lives were dramatically changed because they made the decision to have sex. These examples, although fictional, will help you understand how your whole life can be turned upside down as a result of making the wrong decisions. Those wrong decisions will undoubtedly affect your relationship with Jesus, and as a consequence, you will surely fall into the trap of sexual sin.

Karen was 16 years old; she and her boyfriend had been together for over eight months. They were both Christians and had met at a community church picnic. Everything started out innocently. They actually were both a little shy, and at first barely said anything to each other. Karen was excited because this was her first relationship with a Christian boy. As time went on and they got to know each other better, things started to change. After six months of exclusive dating, Karen and her boyfriend started playing around. They started off kissing each other and touching each other in inappropriate places. They had not had sex yet, but were headed in that direction.

They made a pact that they would not have intercourse. Two months later they took another step. It wasn't long after that until they had done everything. They had broken the pact that they had made. Karen felt so guilty and tried to justify her actions by saying to herself that it was okay to have sex with her boyfriend because they really cared about each other. She felt that they were justified because they were still attending church. Once they started having sex, they wanted to have it more and more. Eventually, Karen's relationship with God became nonexistent. She hated going to church and she never prayed.

There was nothing more for Karen and her boyfriend to look forward to in their relationship. Things were so different now. It seemed that everything was going wrong in her life. Her boyfriend would come over, and they would have sex. That was it. She and her boyfriend were fighting constantly. Sex was ruining their relationship. It was ruining their lives. Her relationship with her parents went downhill. Karen knew that she was hurting her parents. God was truly showing her that she was disobeying him and he was not pleased. So finally she repented. To Karen, repenting felt so good. Her life was so much better. Karen and her boyfriend continued to date, but decided that they would stop having sex. There have been times when they were tempted, but they didn't give in.

Even though you may have made wrong decisions and have traveled down the wrong road at times, God can turn your life around. This story about Tina is sure to help you make the right decision. Tina was seventeen years old when she was ordered by the court to live in a girl's home because she had been in so much trouble at home and at school. The judge ordered her to spend six months in a girl's home. It was during a rap session that Tina made this confession. She said, I only wish I had known more about sex when I was a teenager. If I had only listened to what I heard my parents tell me and what I heard at my teen bible study class, I wouldn't have made some of the mistakes that I made.

I experimented with premarital sex at an early age. I am ashamed to say it, but I don't even recall who my first sexual partner was. I was just living for the moment and not really thinking about my future. It was just all about having fun, or what I thought was fun. My mom kept telling me that all the boys that I was having sex with really didn't love me, but I didn't want to hear what she was saying so I just tuned her out. My friends would tell me different stories about the boys who I was having sex with. They kept warning me to be careful because the boys were not being faithful to me, but I didn't want to hear that either. I wanted to believe that I was the only one.

When I started having sex, my whole attitude changed. I didn't care about school, and making good grades was the last thing on my mind. I realize now that my mom is my best friend, but then, I thought she was my worst enemy. I know now that she was only trying to protect me. I didn't see the point of listening to all those condemning sermons, and I didn't need a preacher to tell me that I was doing wrong. Deep down inside I knew what I was doing was wrong. In an attempt to fool my mother into thinking that I was still involved in church, I would get on the church bus and ride to church, then I would walk off and go to my friend's house; I never made it inside the church.

I often wonder now, 'why didn't someone try to stop me and tell me to come back to church?' I think that way now, but back then, if someone would have tried to stop me I probably would have cursed him or her out. Maybe that's why they didn't stop me. But anyway, I have learned a lot. When you are doing those things, you really don't think about the damage that you are doing to yourself. I think, no I know, that when I started having sex, all my troubles began. I would do anything to be with my boyfriends. When I say anything, I mean anything. I can't tell you how many times I have gotten out of my bedroom window and stayed out all night.

The next morning when my mom didn't see me in my bedroom, she would begin to search the neighborhood looking for me. Sometimes she would find me and other times she wouldn't. Sometimes I would be gone three or four days, and my mom would not know where I was. Oh no, I didn't call her; I was too busy thinking about myself. Because I did selfish things and only thought about myself, I destroyed so many relationships. It got to the point where no one wanted to be around me. It is sad to say, but being sent to a girl's home was a blessing. I know that it was meant as a punishment, but it was truly a blessing.

I have learned about God's forgiveness. I am a Christian now. I still have to mend some other relationships with some of my family members, but thank God that I have the main relationship, and that is with Jesus. I know that a relationship with Jesus is the best relationship that anyone can ever have. It is nice to be in a relationship where I don't have to use my body in a negative way just so I can hear the words: I love you. I don't have to be disrespectful. I don't have to do things to get attention; Jesus gives me all the attention that I need. What I like about this relationship is that Jesus is faithful to me and he loves me for who I am. I know that in some cases experience is the best teacher, but if you can learn from my mistakes, then you will be better off and you won't risk the chance of destroying your relationship with your parents, but most importantly with God."

If you have never invited Jesus into your heart, then you don't have a relationship with him, but you can! Right now! You can stop reading this book at this very moment and ask Jesus to come into your heart, right now! (We will discuss more about God's plan of salvation in chapter ten).

3. Respect

Respect is defined as esteem for, or a sense of worth for a person. The bible teaches us that we should have respect for one another, but we should also have respect for ourselves. Self-respect comes from within. I can't stress enough how important it is to have respect for yourself. My mom was so right in the words that she so eloquently spoke when she said, "You can't expect anyone to have respect for you if you don't have respect for yourself." How can you expect honor, when you don't honor yourself? How can you expect someone to love you, when you don't love yourself? How can you expect someone to cherish you, when you don't cherish yourself? Believe me if you lay down like a doormat, people will walk all over you. You can't demand respect; you have to earn it. If you don't set standards, you won't earn respect from your peers. Remember, "If you don't stand for something you will fall for anything?" Set your standards and stick to them. You don't have to walk around with an "I am a Virgin" sign around your neck, but your friends do need to know what you stand for. A lot of guys in my high school didn't even approach me because they knew that I was committed to my decision.

This is another fictional example to help you understand how not having respect for yourself can lead to a life of disappointment and absolute chaos. Marcy was involved in a relationship with an older guy named Jim. She absolutely adored him, and was so in love. She had such high hopes of marrying him one day. Jim even told her that one day they would get married, but for the time being they should just live together, so that they could see if things would work out before they got married.

Marcy was content with "practicing being married" for the time being, but she lived for the day that they would get married. It seemed every conversation that they had always ended with the topic of them getting married. After a period of time living together, it became very obvious that things had changed, at least for Jim. Marcy and Jim had very different agendas. Marcy still wanted to get married, but Jim seemed satisfied with the way things were. Marcy often said that she sometimes would get frustrated because it was very apparent that Jim was using her. He didn't like to talk about their relationship anymore.

Marcy brought the subject up one day when they were on a date. She asked him when they were going to get married. His reply was "Why should I buy the cow when I am getting the milk for free?" Jim didn't see the need to commit to Marcy because he was already getting everything that he wanted. I am sure you have heard of that phrase before. Have you ever taken the time to think about what it really means?

If you are in a relationship and you are already having sex, chances are your boyfriend is not going to commit to you because he is getting everything that he wants from you, without having to make a commitment. Why should Jim make a commitment to Marcy when he is getting all the benefits that come along with having a fulfilling committed relationship? You don't have to subject yourself to this kind of treatment. You are worth being committed to. Don't settle for anything less because you deserve the best!

Now that we have discussed the three R's, let's discuss other reasons why you should wait to have sex until you are married. Avoiding the responsibility of becoming a parent before you are ready is a practical reason to wait until you are married to have sex. Being a parent is one of the most challenging, but yet rewarding responsibilities one can have. Raising a baby isn't easy under the best circumstances, but it makes it even harder as a teenager. It adds unneeded stress. Having a baby changes your life forever.

Just ask Mary; she is another example that I created to make it easier for you to understand how important it is to make the right decisions. Mary met her boyfriend when she was a freshman in high school. They dated for about a year and had always talked about "being together forever" and getting married one day. Mary and her boyfriend were sexually active and were naïve in thinking that she could ever get pregnant, but they were wrong.

Mary noticed that she was becoming tired a lot, and she was often sick. Missing a lot of days of school, Mary's parents became concerned about what was wrong with their daughter. Her mom made an appointment for Mary to see the doctor. Mary was given a pregnancy test, which revealed that she was indeed pregnant. She thought to herself "How could this have happened?" She and her boyfriend had always practiced safe sex, by using a condom. Mary didn't realize that condoms aren't one hundred percent effective and sometimes they fail. Mary and her boyfriend should have known that the best way to prevent a pregnancy is abstinence.

Mary's parents were very upset and hurt that she became pregnant, but they gave her the support that she needed. Although she knew that she had the support of her parents, the responsibility of raising the baby would be hers. Mary knew that her life would be different but she wasn't really prepared for all the changes that she would have to endure. She knew that she would not be able to hang out with her friends whenever she wanted to, unless she took her baby with her. Mary was afraid that her friends would get tired of having a baby tagging along everywhere they went. She also feared that her friends would eventually stop hanging around with her.

Mary had her baby and shortly after, she was force to get a job. She had to work very hard to support her baby. It was difficult trying to balance going to work and school at the same time. Mary was used to getting up and getting herself ready in the mornings, but now she had to get up three hours earlier to make sure that her baby was fed, changed, and ready to go to the daycare center. This was a big adjustment for Mary. Her boyfriend was not supportive of her at all, because he felt that she should have had an abortion.

All of Mary's assumptions came true. Her friends stopped hanging around. Her boyfriend denied that the baby was his and stopped coming over to her house. Mary's parents did help some, but they reminded her that the baby was her responsibility. Mary learned a very important lesson, which changed her life forever. She never dreamed that her life would change so drastically. Mary never thought that this would happen to her. She is a prime example of how engaging in premarital sex can change your life.

Another reason for waiting to have sex is to avoid contracting a sexually transmitted disease. When you are involved sexually, you take a chance on contracting an STD, which can be very devastating. Although there are some diseases that can be cured, there are others that are incurable. Sex is not worth contracting a STD.

Stacy was a young girl who contracted a sexually transmitted disease, and it killed her. She was a typical teenage girl who loved to talk on the phone, and go out with her friends. One of her favorite past times was shopping with her mom. Stacy was an above average student, she participated in school activities like cheerleading, Drama Club, Beta Club and Interact Club. Stacy seemed to be the all around teenage girl. Although she had an active life, she still managed to make time for a boyfriend. Her boyfriend, Mike, was equally active in school activities, and he was also an above average student.

Stacy and Mike had a close relationship. They both knew that it was wrong, to have sex, but they had it anyway. Mike was a little more experienced sexually than Stacy was. At the beginning of their relationship he confided in Stacy and told her that he had two other partners before her. Stacy was okay with that, even though Mike was her first sexual partner. Both Stacy and Mike were well educated on sexually transmitted diseases and how they are contracted. They had attended a sex education class together that was offered at their school in the spring, but with all the other things going on in their lives, they rarely had time to talk about things like STD's.

Who wants to talk about STDs anyway? They had more important issues on their mind. They had to plan their lives together and make preparations for the future. It was agreed upon that one day they would inevitably go to college together, graduate, get married and start their family. He would major in microbiology and she would major in civil engineering. They seemed to have it all planned out. But life, as it sometimes does, put a glitch in their plans.

Three weeks after Stacy had sexual intercourse with Mike, she noticed sores in her mouth. She didn't make a big deal about it because it didn't hurt and it eventually went away. She didn't give much thought about the sores after that. Later on, Stacy broke out in a rash all over her body. This alarmed her a little bit, but not enough to get checked out. She again pushed it in the back of her mind, and thought of all the reasons where the rash could have come from. She thought of everything except an STD.

The sores reappeared, but this time they were not only in her mouth, but also in her vagina, and buttocks. Now she was convinced that she needed to go to the doctor. Stacy decided that she would go to her local health department to be checked. She asked Mike to go with her. She was sure that it was nothing, but she wanted him to go just for support. She thought the doctor would just write her a prescription and tell her to get plenty of rest. Unfortunately, that was not the case for Stacy. The doctor diagnosed her as having syphilis. Because she didn't get the necessary treatment at the onset of her symptoms, she was now in stage two. Syphilis germs had been multiplying and spreading throughout her body. The doctor did write her a prescription, but that was not the end of everything. As time went on, Stacy got sicker and eventually had to be hospitalized. The disease had started to affect her brain, kidneys and her muscles. Stacy eventually died from syphilis.

Since Mike was her only sexual partner, he was tested and it was confirmed that he too had syphilis. He had contracted syphilis from the girl who he had previously dated. Mike passed it on to Stacy. Stacy did not live to see her dreams fulfilled. If you and I could talk to Stacy now, I am almost sure that she would tell you not to make the same mistake that she made. It is not worth it! Stacy lost her life because she did not follow God's instructions for sex. Don't let what happened to her happen to you.

I hope that you have learned something from the stories that you have just read. In addition to the stories, I wanted to provide a few strategies that you can use to help you wait until marriage to have sex.

Strategies that you can use to help you maintain your virginity

> **Make a commitment to wait**. Making a commitment is a personal decision. If you do not make a commitment, then you are likely to have sex.

> **Find a friend who has the same commitment -** Having someone who has made the same commitment makes it easier to stay committed to your decision. You can be support for one another.

> **Say "NO" with confidence** - You should be proud of the decision that you have made to wait. You have the right to say no. Others should understand that your "no" means "no".

> **Set standards well in advance** - You must set standards well in advance so that others will know where you stand.

> **Let your decision be known** - You should let your friends know about your decision to wait and try to encourage them to make the same decision.

> **Do not get involved with someone you think might try to pressure you** - A true friend will not try to persuade you to do something that goes against what you believe. If they are trying to convince you to do something that is not right, then you do not need to associate with them.

> **Avoid risky sexually explicit movies, music and TV programs -** It is not a secret that some television programs and certain types of music have a negative impact on the decisions that you make.

> **Avoid using alcohol or drugs** - Alcohol and drugs could have an adverse affect on the decisions that you make. Alcohol and drugs affect your ability to control your actions. Your chances of having sex increase if alcohol

and drugs are involved.

> **Plan your dates** - You should make plans ahead of time about where you will go on each date. Preparation is the key. Be prepared for your dates.

> **Avoid risky places and situations -** Don't get involved in situations that will cause you to be tempted. Don't allow yourself to be placed in compromising positions. You will probably be more tempted to have sex if you are alone with your boyfriend than if you were with a group of your friends.

STOP Method for Maintaining Your Virginity

S - Submit to God's will.

T - Talk to God and to others who will encourage you to keep your virginity

O - Obey the Word of God

P - Pray to God and ask him for strength to maintain your virginity.

Reflection

1. What does God say about sex?
2. Why should you wait to have sex?

_____

_____

_____

_____

_____

_____

Chapter 3

Is It Too Late For Me?

So what if you have already had sex? Is it too late for you? The answer is absolutely "No"! It is never too late to start over. You can make a decision to stop having sex now and start practicing abstinence. You can reclaim your virginity. You can start over and make a commitment to not have sex until you are married. You can be renewed. You don't have to be bound down by past mistakes.

Maybe you have someone in your life that can't seem to let go of your past. It seems all that they can think about is what you have done wrong. Or maybe you are holding on to your past because you have made so many mistakes and feel as though you can't be forgiven. Well, you can be forgiven, and now is the time for you to be set free. It doesn't matter what you have done in the past. God will forgive you if you repent. To repent means to feel remorse for what you have done. The bible says in *I John 1:9, "If we confess our sins, he is faithful and just to forgive us our sins and to cleanse us from all unrighteousness."*

God says that when He forgives our sins He will never remember them again. Unlike Satan who constantly reminds you of your past, God will never bring your past mistakes back up ever again. Satan's job is to steal, kill and destroy (John 10:10). He wants to steal your joy, kill your spirit, and destroy your mind. Satan, the master of mind games, realizes that if he can get your mind stuck on your past, then you will take your focus off of Jesus. But your past is exactly that – the past. No matter what Satan tells you, **you can be renewed. You are a new person! You are not the same person anymore! All is forgiven! Today is a new day in your life!**

Don't let Satan destroy your life by controlling your mind with thoughts about your past. Satan likes to accuse you and make you feel guilty for your past mistakes so that he can keep you down. He wants you to be discouraged. He hopes to keep you so low and so down on yourself that you will never be what God has called you to be. If you concentrate on all the things that you have done wrong in your past, you will never be able to enjoy the bright future that God has promised you.

I challenge you to direct your attention to the one who created you, the one who holds your future, the one who can, and will forgive you. In the past you may have believed that some of the things that you have done were so bad that you can't be forgiven, but now you know that God will forgive you and accept you with open arms. Isn't it good to know that no matter what you have done, you can start over? In order to get a fresh start, you must repent of your past sins. Below you will find the steps to repentance.

Steps to Repentance

1. Become Godly sorry for the sins that you have committed.
2. Confess to God the sins that you have committed.
3. Ask for forgiveness
4. Turn away from sin
5. Receive forgiveness

Become Godly sorry for the sins that you have committed.

To be Godly sorry goes beyond being sorry because you were caught in your sin, but it is a sincere feeling of betrayal against God. Worldly sorrow is feeling sorrow for getting caught and not feeling sorrow for the sin that you committed. There is a big difference between Godly sorrow and worldly sorrow. Godly sorrow leads to repentance. *"Now I rejoice, not that ye were made sorry, but that ye sorrowed to repentance: for ye were made sorry after a godly manner...for godly sorrow worketh repentance to salvation...but the sorrow of the world worketh death"* (2 Corinthians 7: 9-10).

Confess to God the sin that you have committed.

Acknowledge that you have sinned and fallen short of God's glory. You must confess to God the sin that you have committed.

Ask for forgiveness

Once you have confessed to God the sin(s) that you have committed, you must ask God for forgiveness. You need to be sincere when you ask him for forgiveness. Asking for forgiveness helps bring a sense of peace and harmony between you and God.

Turn away from sin

Turning away from sin is a very important step. It is not enough to become Godly sorry, confess your sin, and ask for forgiveness, but you must also turn away from sin. Once you have stopped the sin, you must make a commitment to never do that sin again.

Receive forgiveness

Accept the fact that God has forgiven you for the sins that you have committed. Pray and ask God to give you the strength to keep you from sinning.

Reflection

1. Is it ever too late to start over?
2. What are the steps to repentance?

_____

_____

_____

_____

_____

_____

Chapter 4

FACING TEMPTATION

Temptation is defined as the act of trying to persuade (especially to do evil) to entice or induce. Temptation occurs when the opportunity is presented to do what we know is wrong, whether against God, others, or ourselves. Everyone faces temptation at one time or another in his or her life. Each of us is tempted at different levels. Your temptation might be eating the wrong kinds of food, like junk food. Your friend's temptation might be dealing with being involved in a harmful lifestyle.

Regardless of who we are, where we are from, or where we live, we all have been, and will be, tempted. Being tempted is not wrong; it is when we give in to our temptation that it turns into sin. Again, being tempted is not a sin, but the action that follows behind it is what results in sin.

Fighting temptation is a battle between focusing on the desires of the flesh versus doing what is right. This battle cannot be fought alone and it cannot be won relying on your own strength. Some people have the misconception that if they possess willpower and personal stamina that they will be able to win against temptation. Relying on your own strength is setting yourself up for failure. *Ephesians 6:12-13 says, "For we wrestle not against flesh and blood but against principalities, against powers, against the ruler of darkness of this world, against spiritual wickedness in high places. Wherefore take unto you the whole armour of God that ye may be able to withstand in the evil day and having done all to stand."*

Jesus understands how it feels to be tempted, he was tempted himself, so you are not alone. Jesus was tempted, but he never sinned. The good news for us is we don't have to sin either, because Jesus has planned a way of escape for us to get out of temptation. . *I Corinthians 10:13 says, "There hath no temptation taken you but such as is common to man: but God is faithful, who will not suffer you to be tempted above that ye are able, but will with the temptation also make a way to escape that ye may be able to bear it."*

Temptation always involves a choice - will we obey God or give in to our own desires? It is always best to obey God. Although your flesh may be leading you in another direction, it is to your benefit to listen to the voice of God and not yield to temptation. There is a blessing in fighting temptation. *James 1:12-16 says "Blessed is the man that endureth temptation: for when he is tried, he shall receive the crown of life, which the Lord hath promised to them that love him."*

We can learn a lot from Joseph and how he avoided temptation (Genesis 39). Joseph was a righteous man, and the Lord blessed him. When Potiphar saw that Joseph was blessed by God and was successful in everything that he did, he appointed him as overseer. This meant that Joseph was responsible for Potiphar's house and everything that he owned. Potiphar's wife was attracted to Joseph because he was handsome.

She tried to tempt Joseph by asking him to go to bed with her. But Joseph refused. Day after day she would ask Joseph to go to bed with her. But Joseph always refused. One day when Joseph went into the house to take care of his responsibilities, none of the men who worked in the house were there. When Potiphar's wife saw that she was alone with Joseph, she grabbed a hold of his cloak (coat), and tried to coax him to come to her. Joseph pulled away and ran, leaving her holding his cloak. Potiphar's wife called the men of the house and showed them Joseph's cloak. She told them that Joseph had tried to have sex with her, but she screamed. After she screamed, Joseph ran away. Of course Potiphar's wife was not telling the truth. Joseph refused to give in to his temptation. He used wisdom in his decision to run from her and as a result he avoided yielding to temptation.

If you are ever in a situation like Joseph, you too may have to run away. Don't be afraid or ashamed to run from temptation, no matter what others may say about you. Avoiding temptation shows that you have respect for yourself and respect for God.

Reflection

1. What does it mean to be tempted?
2. What does the word of God teach us about temptation?
3. What action will you take the next time you are tempted?
4. What can we learn from Joseph?
5. What scripture reference can you use when facing temptation?

_____

_____

_____

_____

_____

Chapter 5

ABSTINENCE

So far, in previous chapters we have discussed why you should wait to have sex. In this chapter you will learn about the word that defines what waiting actually means, and that word is abstinence. What is abstinence? Sexual abstinence is the avoidance of sexual activity. Abstinence is the only sure way to avoid getting pregnant. Sexually transmitted diseases may also be avoided, if one practices abstinence.

Choosing to be abstinent is completely up to you, but there are some disadvantages if you choose not to be. One who makes the decision to have sex before marriage risks having a lifetime of emotional baggage and broken relationships. As mentioned earlier, abstinence is the only sure way to avoid getting pregnant or contracting a sexually transmitted disease. Another beneficial reason for practicing abstinence until you are married is having respect for your future spouse.

God designed sex to be a very intimate experience between a husband and a wife. Having sex with someone before marriage, takes away from the gift of purity that you could have given. Your ability to save yourself tells your future spouse that you had the will power and the desire to wait for him or her.

To help you with your commitment to remain abstinent until marriage, I have written the *Abstinence Pledge*. The *Abstinence*

Pledge is a source of encouragement for you and your friends. Ask a friend to make a stand with you, and both of you should refer to it as often as possible. The pledge should serve as a daily reminder of the commitment that you have made.

Abstinence Pledge

I was created in the image of God's son Jesus Christ. I am fearfully and wonderfully made. The sole purpose of my existence is to glorify God. I will glorify God with my mind, body and soul. I acknowledge that my body belongs to God, therefore I will abstain from fleshly lusts which war against my soul (I Peter 2:11). I pledge to remain faithful to God, my future spouse, and myself by not having sex until marriage.

_____   _____

Your Name   Date

_____   _____

Your Friend's Name   Date

Reflection

1. What is abstinence?
2. Why is it important to remain abstinent until marriage?

_____

_____

_____

_____

_____

_____

Chapter 6

CHOICES! CHOICES! CHOICES!

We all have to make choices every day of our lives. What will we eat for breakfast: Cheerios or Frosted Flakes? What will we wear to school: blue jeans or capris? Who will be your friend? What movie will you see? Will it be a mystery or a comedy? There will come a time in your life when you will have to make more profound decisions such as: whether or not you will try drugs? When and with whom you will have sex? Will you go to college, technical school or immediately join the workforce? We all, at some point in our lives, will have to make choices. The choices that you make today will affect your tomorrow.

You have the power to choose. You are in control of your destiny. You can make wise choices like staying in school and getting a good education, and avoiding using drugs and not engaging in sexual activities. You can also make bad choices and take the road that leads to destruction. It's a decision that you will have to make. Below are some of the issues that you very well may have to face one day.

Friends

Friends are very important to have and we all need them.

You must be very careful when you choose your friends because they can, and will, influence you. *Proverbs 22:24-25 says "Make no friendship with an angry man and with a furious man do not go, lest you learn his ways and set a snare for your soul."* You learn from your friends. You pick up their habits and sayings, their likes and dislikes. They influence your attitude and your way of thinking. If your friend has bad habits or a bad attitude, eventually you will develop bad habits and a bad attitude. That is why it is so important to have godly friends, so that you can develop godly habits. If you associate with ungodly friends, then they will corrupt you.

I *Corinthians 15:33* says, *"Do not be deceived: Evil company corrupts good habits."* Don't be fooled, the evil that your friends do will soon corrupt your good habits. Have you ever been warned to watch the company that you keep? If you have, take heed to the warning, and if you haven't then consider yourself warned.   Your friends should draw you closer to God rather than away from him. It is important to God that you choose your friends wisely. Proverbs 13:20 says, *"He who walks with wise men will be wise, but the companion of fools will be destroyed."* God has called you to walk godly and keep away from sin. If you have friends who have a negative impact on you, then you need to get away from those friends.

Dating/Marriage

Most people start relationships based on how a person looks. However, it is not enough just to be attracted to a guy, you need to know what is on the inside. You should get to know a person before you commit to dating him. As you get to know him, you might find that he is okay to date, or you might find that he is a wolf in sheep's clothing. He might be attractive on the outside, but his inner qualities might not be so attractive. When you are considering whom you will date, look beyond the outer qualities and look within. Physical appearances change, but inner qualities last a lifetime. Set some standards and only date those who share your beliefs.

Perhaps at this point you aren't thinking about whom you will marry, but one day you will. Who you marry will have a lasting effect on your life, which is why it is so important that you make a wise choice. I had an aunt who told me to never date anyone who does not possess the qualities that I would look for in someone I would marry. She said, "set some standards and if he does not meet the standards that you have set, then you shouldn't date him and you most certainly shouldn't marry him."

2 Corinthians 6:14 says, "Do not be yoked together with unbelievers, for what do righteousness and wickedness have in common? Or what fellowship can light have with darkness." You should not get emotionally involved with someone you will not marry. I can't count the number of my friends who got involved with guys and believed that they could change him. A person first has to want to change, and then only God can change them. Don't get involved in a relationship that you will feel obligated to play the role of savior, which means you are trying to save the world all by yourself.

Alcohol/Drugs

If you haven't had to make a choice concerning alcohol and drugs, you probably will one day. Alcohol and drugs affect your central nervous system, which can cause you to have poor judgment. If you don't have good judgment, you might find yourself in a compromising situation. You are more likely to be sexually active and to have unsafe, unprotected sex, when you make the choice of using alcohol and drugs. Not only can these substances impair your judgment, they may also result in unwanted pregnancies, and sexually transmitted diseases. Now you have at your disposal a wealth of knowledge to help you make the right choice.

Sex

Sex is a big deal. It is not just the physical act itself that you should take into account, but the emotional aspect as well. You have a choice to either have sex now or save it for marriage. Just because your friends are having sex doesn't necessarily mean that it is the right thing for you to do. Don't give in to peer- pressure about sex. Your friends don't have the right to tell you what to do with your body or when to do it. It is your decision. Remember: one moment of passion can cause a lifetime of pain.

You Decide

➤ You alone can decide whom you will choose to be your boyfriend.

➤ You alone can decide to control your sexual desires.

➤ You alone can decide how best to let others know you will not engage in any kind of sexual relationship before marriage.

➤ You alone can choose not to allow others to pressure you into doing things that you don't feel are right for you.

➤ You alone can decide not to drink alcohol, do drugs or anything else, which might cause you to make bad decisions.

➤ You alone can decide whom you will marry.

➤ You alone can decide to remain faithful and true to the one you marry.

Reflection

1. What are some of the choices that you will have to make?
2. What are some possible consequences that you will have to face if you make bad choices?

_____

_____

_____

_____

_____

_____

Chapter 7

Words Of Wisdom

Don't Rush Life

The time will come when you will have the opportunity to experience new things. If you do everything now, what will you have to look forward to in the future? Life is like going to school, because it seems as though they're both divided into levels. During each level you are expected to learn certain bits of information, and you must follow through each grade level. You can't expect to leave kindergarten and go immediately into the second grade; so it is with the order of life.

Life comes in stages, and during each stage we are to grasp more and more knowledge. You are born an infant, then you become a toddler, preschooler, adolescent, young adult and then an adult. You can't expect to go from a preschooler to an adult because that is not the order of things; so don't rush it. There is a great deal of responsibility that comes with being an adult, so enjoy being a teenager while you can.

Enjoy Being A Teenager

You might not understand everything about life, so I am sure that you have a lot of questions. Contrary to what you believe or how you feel, you have not been cursed. You can live a victorious fulfilled life as a teenager. You will get through this phase of your life, I promise. You often hear about the things that you can't do, but there are positive things that you can get involved with that will not be hazardous to your health and will not hinder your walk with the Lord. One of the most important positive things that you can do is to develop a relationship with Jesus. The closer you draw to God; the closer he will draw to you. During these challenging times, find out who you are in the Lord and celebrate this season in your life! Embrace every opportunity to celebrate who you are.

Don't Get Caught Up In The Moment

It is dangerous to make a decision without thinking it through carefully first. Many times you are confronted with problems, and without thinking, you make irrational decisions. Then later, when you've had time to think about what actually happened, you regret the choices that you made. It is important to remember to use wisdom in every decision that you have to make. Whatever decision you make, whether it is good or bad, you will have to live with the consequences.

Be Yourself

Have you ever tried to imitate someone else, only to find out that you couldn't be that person? The reason that it was difficult for you to pretend to be someone else is because God made you who you are. You are unique and very special in his eyes. Your were created for a specific purpose that only you are able to fulfill. Take pride in who you are and use what God has given you to be the best that you can be.

Make A Difference In Someone Else's Life

Always purpose in your heart to make difference for someone else. Sometimes it is the smaller things in life that make the most difference, so don't focus on the big act of service all of the time.

If you center your attention on meeting the needs of others, you will be blessed in returned.

Obey Your Parents

Ephesians 6:2 says, "*Children obey your parents in the Lord for this is right.*" It may seem as though your parents don't understand you, or you might think that they don't know what they are talking about, but the bible says that you are suppose to obey them. I will admit that things have changed since your parents were teenagers, but they remember what it was like to be a teenager and they understand what you are going through. You may be aware of some mistakes that your parents made when they were teenagers, but that is not a reason for you to make those same mistakes. Your parents want what is best for you. Show them the respect and love that they deserve.

Trust God With Your Future

The Bible says, in *Jeremiah 29:11* "*For I know the plans that I have for you' declares the Lord, 'plans to prosper you and not to harm you, plans to give you hope and a future.*" God already has your future mapped out. Before the beginning of time, God predestined everything that would take place in your life. God knows everything about you. It makes sense to follow the blueprints that God has already orchestrated for your life.

Believe in yourself

You will always have critics, not everyone will believe in you. However, you must believe in yourself. It doesn't matter what people say about you, it is what you say and believe about yourself. People don't have to believe in you in order for your dreams to come true. Don't lose focus of your dreams. Believe that you can maximize your potential and achieve any goal that you have set for yourself. It doesn't matter from what walk of life you are from, you can achieve your goals if you set your mind to it.

Words to Live By

If you can dream it, you can achieve it.
Do the best you can, in all that you do.
Set high goals and make them happen.
Treat others like you want to be treated.
Live life to the fullest.

Reflection

1. How can you apply the words of wisdom to your life?
2. How can you help a friend understand the words of wisdom?

_____

_____

_____

_____

_____

_____

Chapter 8

SELF ESTEEM

What is self-esteem? According to the American Heritage College Dictionary, self-esteem is pride in oneself and self-respect. Either you have a healthy self-esteem or an unhealthy self-esteem. Some people refer to it as high or low self-esteem. A person with a high or healthy self-esteem is confident, with whom they are. They are able to accept and learn from their own mistakes. They don't take themselves too seriously, and they are able to laugh at themselves. Setbacks and obstacles don't easily defeat them. A person with a low or unhealthy self-esteem is just the opposite. They are not confident and not happy with themselves, and they are easily defeated.

We have all had moments when we didn't feel confident, or there have been times when we have been afraid to try new things. We have even had moments when we didn't think that we looked our best. Let's face it girls, we are always concerned about our appearance. We do like to look good, and that's okay. We should always strive to be the best and to look our best, but it is important to understand that who we are is not based on how we look or how smart we are. What counts is on the inside. Having a healthy self-esteem does not mean that you have to be perfect. There will be times when you will doubt yourself or even make a mistake. We all have shortcomings or faults. The bible even tells us in *Romans 3:23 that we have all fallen short of the glory of God.*

Your self-esteem should be based on how you feel about yourself and not what others say about you. More importantly, your self-esteem should be based on how God feels about you. God thinks you are special. He accepts you just the way you are and he loves you unconditionally. If you really focus on how God feels about you, you can't help but to have a healthy self-esteem.

Unfortunately, there are some girls whose self-esteem is not healthy. It could be because they have suffered some type of hardship or may have been in an unhealthy relationship that caused them to develop a low self-esteem. There was once a girl named Tamara. She grew up in an abusive home, where there were always fights between her mother and father. Tamara's father was an alcoholic, although he would never admit it. Because he was in denial, he would not seek the help that he needed.

He was very abusive to her mother and to her sisters and brothers. There were several occasions when she witnessed her mother being beaten, sometimes it was because of something as simple as what she cooked for dinner, or it could be what they usually fought about: the lack of money. It always seemed that they would run out of money before they paid all of the bills. It was during those times that Tamara's dad seemed the most stressed. He would often times come home in a foul mood and anything could set him off.

Everybody tried to stay out of his way, but he always managed to find something to fuss about. It always seemed that Tamara was an open target for his rude comments. He often told her that she was fat and ugly and that she would never amount to anything. He told her that he hated to be around her, and not only did he say it, but he showed it too. She often heard "You'll never get a boyfriend because nobody likes you." He never had anything good to say to her, only one put down after another.

Tamara heard so many negative comments until she finally

started believing them. She believed that she would never amount to anything. She didn't have enough confidence in herself to believe that she could achieve any of her goals, so she rarely put forth the effort to try to do anything. She didn't think that she was valuable. Following in the footsteps of her dad, she often ridiculed herself. She was her own worst enemy. She never had anything good to say about herself. She quickly adapted to the feelings of being unloved. Tamara really believed that her dad didn't love her. She thought there was no way that he could love her because of the way he treated her. Like everyone else, Tamara longed to be loved and accepted. She was willing to get the love anyway that she could get.

One day she met a guy named CJ. He wasn't the best looking guy, and he wasn't very nice either. He treated her like her father did. He would insult her and sometimes he was physically abusive to her. Tamara didn't really like the way that she was treated but she was happy to have a boyfriend. Tamara's boyfriend eventually started asking her to do things like smoke and have sex. She didn't really want to do those things, but she did them just to keep him. She was so glad to have a boyfriend, and she did all she could to make him happy.

Does the life of Tamara sound familiar? Unfortunately, like Tamara, a lot of girls have low self-esteem and they subject themselves to demeaning behavior. No one has to be like Tamara. You can start now developing a healthy self-esteem. I want you to take a few minutes and think of at least three things that you like about yourself. Now write them down.

1._____

2._____

3._____

Now find a mirror, and look at yourself and repeat what you have written down. You might feel silly at first, but keep on doing it until you begin to feel better about yourself. Soon, you won't need to look in a mirror, because how you feel about yourself will be safe and secure deep within your soul.

Things To Remember

You deserve to be treated with respect.

You don't have to accept any demeaning treatment.

You are beautiful from the inside out.

You are unique.

Your self-esteem comes from within.

Reflection

1. What can cause you to have a poor self-esteem?
2. How important is it to have a healthy self-esteem?
3. What can you do to encourage a friend to have a positive self-esteem?

_____

_____

_____

_____

_____

_____

Chapter 9

Peer Pressure

Peer pressure is when friends persuade you into doing something that you do not want to do. There are two types of peer pressure, negative and positive. Negative or bad peer pressure is when you are pressured into doing things that are harmful. Positive or good peer pressure is when you may be pressured by friends to not make a bad decision and to do what is right. Regardless of your race, nationality, socioeconomic status, or demographical location, we all face some type of pressure.

We have all been pressured by our friends to do things, good or bad. Your friends might persuade you to do positive things such as join a school club or team, to go to church, or to make good grades. On the other hand, your peers might try to persuade you to get involved in things that are not good for you, like trying drugs, alcohol, skipping class or having sex. You might feel pressured to have sex because you think that everybody is doing it or you feel as though you have to do it to be in the "in crowd". You will be affected by peer pressure, but it is up to you how you handle it. You don't have to give in. It is not always easy to stand up and say "no" especially when you are the only one saying "no," but you can do it.

Unfortunately, you will always have someone who will try

to pressure you into doing bad things. For this reason, you have to be prepared so that you will know how to deal with the pressure. I can remember when I was younger I felt pressured to do what some of my friends were doing. I wanted to be in the "in crowd", and accepted by my peers. It didn't feel good to be laughed at, and called "chicken", but I knew that the things that they were pressuring me to do were not the right choices for me, so I didn't give in. The time will come when you will have to decide whether you are going to stand up for what is right or give in to peer pressure.

It is a good idea to know how you are going to handle peer pressure ahead of time before you are confronted with a situation. Don't wait until someone asks you if you want to have sex before you decide how you feel about having sex. If you have not given much thought to what you believe, when you are confronted with an issue you will be more likely to give in.

How to deal with peer pressure?

It is important to know how to deal with peer pressure. Below are a few suggestions that may help you.

1. Think about what your peers are asking you to do.

Is it wrong? Does it go against what you believe? How will it affect you tomorrow? How will it affect you five years from now? Will your parents approve of what you are doing?

2. Think about what could happen.

What will be the consequences if you give in to peer-pressure? If you have sex, will you get pregnant or contract a sexually transmitted disease?

3. Decide beforehand what you are going to say or do when your peers confront you.

Think ahead so you will not feel led to make a hasty decision. If you don't have something in mind to say, you are more likely to give in.

4. Stick to what you believe.

Don't compromise what you believe in. You may run the risk of being ridiculed by your peers, but don't let that make you give in. Ridicule is a small price to pay when it comes to facing some of the consequences you may encounter, if you give in to peer-pressure.

5. Talk to your mom and dad/ or someone you trust.

Share with your parents what is going on in your life. Tell them about the times that you have been confronted with peer pressure. They have been where you are now. They know how it feels to be pressured. They can help you, maybe more than you think.

Reflection

1. What is peer pressure?
2. What are two types of peer pressure?
3. How are you affected by positive/negative peer pressure?
4. How can you handle peer pressure effectively?

_____

_____

_____

_____

_____

_____

Chapter 10

ACCEPTING JESUS AS LORD AND SAVIOR

My friends, I have an important question that I want to ask you. The answer to this question will determine your joy or sorrow for eternity. The question is: have you invited Jesus into your heart? It is not a question of how good you are or how often you attend church, but are you saved? When you die, are you sure you will go to heaven? You must be saved if you want to go to heaven. God gave us a simple plan so that we can be saved.

Accepting Jesus into your heart is the most important decision that you will ever make in your life. It is more important than the decision to abstain from sex until marriage, it is more important than making the decision to fight against temptation. When you accept Jesus as your savior you will be drawn closer to God, your mind will be opened to the truth, the seed of faith will be planted in your heart and you will be freed from bondage that hinders you from moving forward. Accepting Jesus as your Lord and Savior is the foundation of all other decisions that you will ever have to make. Inviting Jesus into your heart is simple. It is literally as easy as ABC.

A - Admit that you are sinner.

Romans 3:23 says, *"For all have sinned and come short of the glory of God."* We have all sinned.

B - Believe in your heart that God raised Jesus from the dead.

You must believe that Jesus died and rose again for your sins. *John 3:16 says, "For God so loved the world that he gave his only begotten son that whosoever should believe in him should not perish but have everlasting life."*   God loves you so much that he gave his only begotten son so that you and I can be saved from our sins.

C - Confess that Jesus is Lord over your life.

Romans 10:9 says, "That if thou shalt confess with thou mouth the Lord Jesus and shall believe in thine heart that God raised him from the dead thou shalt be saved." It is a matter of believing and confessing.

"Jesus has no respect of person." He will accept anyone. According to Romans 10:13 anyone can be saved. *"For whosoever shall call upon the name of the Lord shall be saved."*

If you want to accept Jesus as your personal Savior, pray this prayer:

Lord Jesus, I believe you are the Son of God. Thank you for dying on the cross for my sins. Please forgive me of my sins and give me the gift of eternal life. I ask you into my life, and heart, and to be my Lord and Savior. It is in your name that I pray. Amen

If you were sincere when you prayed that prayer, congratulations on accepting Jesus as your savior. This is the best decision that you could have ever made!!!! Welcome to the family.

Now that you have accepted Jesus as your Lord and Savior you will need to do certain things so that you can grow spiritually. First, you need to be sure that you read your Bible every day so that you can get to know Christ better. When you read your bible, God has an opportunity to talk to you. Secondly, you need to keep the lines of communication open between you and Jesus by praying. You should always have an active prayer life. When you pray you have the opportunity to talk to Jesus. Thirdly, you should be baptized, and should worship, fellowship, and serve with other Christians in a Bible based church, where the Gospel of Jesus Christ is preached and God's Word is the final authority. Finally, you need to be a witness. Being a witness is like being a spokesperson for Jesus. You should tell others about Jesus and encourage them to invite Jesus into their heart.

Reflection

1. What are the benefits of accepting Jesus as your personal savior?
2. How can you accept Jesus as your personal savior?
3. Once you are saved, what do you need to do to grow spiritually?

_____

_____

_____

_____

_____

_____

Study Guide

This study guide was created primarily as a curriculum for small group study for teens and young adults. The guide includes scenarios, which were designed to stimulate discussions and provoke some soul searching among members of your group. As you read the scenarios, see if you can determine what the person did wrong, what they should have done, or what you would have done if you were in that situation. The question and answer session was included to help you remember the strategies that you've learned, with respect to waiting until marriage to have sex.

Learning From Others

It has been said that experience is the best teacher. That may be true in some cases, but not when it comes to having sex. Sometimes it is best to learn from others' mistakes. Look at the following scenarios and see what you can learn.

Scenario 1

Your friend Mary, who is in the 7th grade, met Gary, who is in the 11th grade. Mary really likes Gary because he is older and he is really cool. Gary can do all of the latest dance moves, and he is so handsome. Every time Mary sees Gary her heart seems to skip a beat. He looks just that good. Gary asked Mary if she wanted to go to a party with him that weekend. Mary said, "Yes, I want to go." She was excited about going to a party with high school students. Everything was going great at the party, until some of the guys started drinking. Gary offered Mary some alcohol. At first she said "No", but after seeing the disappointing look on Gary's face, she decided to take a drink. She definitely didn't want to mess up her chances of being invited to another high school party.

Soon after Mary's third drink, she began to feel a little woozy. She really didn't know what was going on. She definitely was not in any condition to make a wise decision. Recognizing that Mary was intoxicated (drunk), Gary asked her if she wanted to go upstairs. Without any questions asked, Mary agreed to go upstairs with Gary. As they entered the room, Gary told Mary that he really liked her and he wanted to show her just how much. He began to take her clothes off. Without any resistance from Mary, they had sex.

Reflection: What can you learn from the decisions that Mary made?

_____

_____

_____

_____

_____

Scenario 2

Sue's cousin, Beth, invited her to go on a blind date, and she agreed to go. She felt that everything was safe because her cousin knew the guy, and told her that he was okay. They all went on a date together. When Sue saw the guy, she felt that he was the right one for her, because he said all the things that every girl wants to hear. The way he looked into her eyes made her heart melt. It didn't take long for Sue and Tom to find a place where they could be alone. They started kissing first on the lips, then he started kissing her neck, then he rubbed his hand across her thighs, and before long he had unbuttoned her shirt. Guess what happened next? You got it! They had sex. On the very first date, they had sex.

Reflection: Can you name three things that Sue did wrong?

_____

_____

_____

_____

_____

Scenario 3

Regina was so in love with Sam. He made her feel so special. He was the best boyfriend that she had ever had. Regina couldn't see it, but Sam had a lot of character flaws. Regina's mom had told her that she didn't need to see him anymore because he wasn't good for her. You see, ever since Regina had been dating Sam she was starting to be disrespectful to her parents. Her grades were falling behind at school. Regina often brushed her mom off and said that she was old fashioned. Regina's friends even tried to warn her about Sam. She believed that they were jealous of her new love and were envious because she had met Mr. Right and they hadn't. Refusing to listen to anyone or take heed to all the warning signs, Regina continued to date Sam. Sam had been telling Regina that she was the only girl that he loved and that they would always be together. According to Sam, they were a match-made-in-heaven. This was all Regina needed to hear. She continued to date Sam and eventually they started having sex.

In the beginning Regina would insist that Sam wear a condom, but as time passed, it seemed as though he would purposefully forget to bring the condoms. Regina had heard about the dangers of having unprotected sex, but she figured that everything would be okay. Everything was going okay, until oneday Regina found out that Sam was having sex with another girl. When Regina confronted Sam, he beat her up. Regina decided to end the relationship and they went their separate ways. Weeks later, Regina found out that she had contracted AIDS.

Reflection: What would you have done differently if you were in Regina's situation?

_____

_____

_____

_____

_____

Scenario 4

Tammy is 14 years old and she is very curious about sex. Her mother does not talk to her about things like sex, so the little that she does know, she learned from her friends. Her mother has told her that one-day her body will change and she will become a woman, but that was the extent of their "sex talk". Tammy's mother never told her about the importance of waiting until she was married to have sex. With the limited knowledge that she had, Tammy decided to explore and find out what sex was all about. She started dating Mark who she met at the skating rink. For the first couple of months, they took things slow, and then eventually they moved to the next step, until finally they were having sex. Tammy lost her virginity at a friend's house.

Now that Tammy had satisfied her curiosity, she found that sex was not what all her friends said it would be. To be honest, she realized that she didn't really like having sex. Deep down in her heart, Tammy knew that it was not the right time for her to have sex. She felt that she couldn't stop now because her friends would think that she was a "chicken." Since she started having sex she became much more popular with the girls and the boys. The ones that normally wouldn't talk to her, suddenly started being friendly to her. Although Tammy liked being popular, she didn't like the idea of having to have sex to maintain her popularity.

Reflection: If you could give Tammy some advice, what advice would you give her?

_____

_____

_____

_____

_____

_____

Scenario 5

There are two boys, Jim and Greg. Jim thinks that it is wrong to have sex with anyone he is not married to. He has a girlfriend and although his friends are pressuring him, he has decided not to have sex with her. When Jim was thirteen he took the abstinence pledge and is committed to saving sex for marriage. Jim and his girlfriend Tara dated for about a year, until she moved to Texas. As time went on, Jim met another girl named Stephanie. His friends were sure that he would give in to the temptation, and have sex with Stephanie, but he stood firm to his commitment. Eventually Jim asked Stephanie to marry him, and she accepted.

On the other hand, his friend Greg thinks that it is okay to have sex with anyone he wants to. He doesn't see the big deal about saving sex before marriage. Greg has a girlfriend named Michelle, and they are involved sexually. Greg promised Michelle that he would never cheat on her, but two months after they started dating, he met a girl named Gina and they started having sex too. As time went on, Greg met another girl named Jennifer, and they also are having sex. Greg is a poor excuse for a boyfriend, but the reality is, there are a lot of Gregs in the world and not nearly enough Jims, and that is unfortunate.

Reflection: What are the benefits of following Jim's example? What are the dangers of following Greg's example? Explain your answer.

_____

_____

_____

_____

_____

_____

Scenario 6

Becky started having sex when she was 14 years old. Although she had taken a health class at school and had learned about the dangers of having multiple sex partners, she really didn't take it serious. She also didn't see the importance of saving sex for marriage.

One-day Becky's friend, Liz invited her to go to a teen camp meeting with her. While attending the camp, Becky learned about the importance of living a life for Christ. She learned that God was not pleased with the life that she was living. God did not like the fact that Becky was having sex. At the end of the last session, Becky talked to the camp director, and told her that she wanted to invite Jesus into her heart and she also wanted to reclaim her virginity. That day Becky accepted Jesus as her savior and she made a commitment to save sex until she was married.

Reflection: What do you think happened at the teen camp meeting that empowered Becky to reclaim her virginity and encouraged her to give her life to Christ?

_____

_____

_____

_____

_____

QUESTIONS AND ANSWERS

1. What if I have already been involved sexually; is it too late for me?

   No, it is never too late to start over. You can always make a commitment to stop being involved sexually and wait until you are married.

2. What if I don't want to have sex, but my boyfriend does?

   You should talk to your boyfriend and tell him that you don't want to have sex and the reasons why. If he can live with your decision, then continue the relationship, but if he can't then you should end the relationship.

3. How can I convince my boyfriend not to pressure me into having sex?

   Tell your boyfriend how it makes you feel when he pressures you. If he is considerate of your feel-

ings, then he should stop. If he does not stop and
you continue to be in a relationship with him,
then you will just have to be firm in telling him
no.

4. What are things that I can do to keep my mind off
   sex?

   You can get involved in extracurricular activities such as basketball, track, softball, and other
   healthy activities. You can also get involved in
   church activities that involve the youth.

5. What if my boyfriend forced me to have sex?

   Nobody has the right to force you to do anything
   that you don't want to do. If your boy friend has
   forced you to have sex, you should tell your parents, and they will contact the proper authorities.

6. Do I have to tell my friends about my decision to
   wait?

   This is a decision that you should be proud of.
   However you don't necessarily have to tell your
   friends about your decision, if you don't feel com-
   fortable in telling them.

7. How can I encourage my friends to wait to have sex?

   First, you can encourage them by setting a good
   example before them. You can tell them about the

rewards of waiting. You can establish a support team, and encourage your friends to wait. You all can make a pact not to have sex.

8. What should I do if my friends are pressuring me to change my decision?

Be firm in your decision to wait until you are married. Don't give in to the pressure. Explain to them how it makes you feel when they pressure you.

9. What if my friends didn't choose to wait, can we still be friends?

Yes, you can still be friends, as long as being their friend doesn't cause you to be tempted to change your decision.

10. How can I fight the pressure to have sex?

One of the best mechanisms that I have found to be effective is prayer. You can pray and ask God to give you the strength not to give in and have sex. Also, be mindful of the things that you are involved in and whom you associate with.

11. Where can I go to get support and encouragement to help me keep my commitment?

You can go to your parents, or your local church, or an organization that focuses on abstinence for support.

12. Can the way I dress affect the way others view me?

Clothes are the way that we package ourselves. It is how we show whom we are and what we think of ourselves. If you dress in clothes that emphasize your sexuality, you are sending the wrong message.

13. Can being abstinent help me focus in school?

Yes, being abstinent can be helpful to you in school. You are not confronted with the emotional and physical pressure that comes along with being sexually active. This allows you to have a clear mind and be able to focus on important issues.

14. Why do people want to have sex?

People have different reasons for wanting to have sex, but ultimately   people want to have it because sex feels good. It is an expression of love. It makes people feel closer and it makes the marriage relationship special.

15. What kinds of problems can premarital sex cause?

Premarital sex can cause physical, spiritual and emotional problems. It can cause an unwanted pregnancy or the contraction of a sexually transmitted disease. Emotionally, it can cause depression, anxiety, insecurity, fear of commitment and

abandonment. Having premarital sex can cause your relationship with God to be destroyed.

16. Is abstinence realistic?

Yes, being abstinent is realistic. It is normal and practical. Exercising willpower to abstain from the moment of passion and excitement that sex can bring can be a reality.

17. Does abstinence mean just saying no?

No, there is more to abstinence than just saying no. You must also promote the concept of abstinence by encouraging others to wait until marriage to have sex.

18. Isn't abstinence just for religious groups?

No, for some, remaining abstinent has everything to do with religion. For others, abstinence is chosen for health reasons. Whatever the case, there are dangers associated with having sex before marriage.

19. How can you practice abstinence?

You can practice abstinence by exercising will power, and using the various strategies that you have learned by reading this book to help.

20. Is abstinence difficult?

For some it is difficult. It really depends on your approach to abstinence. If you are grounded in your decision and avoid situations that could involve sexual activity, then it is much easier.

21. What are the challenges for people who want to abstain?

Peer pressure is the most common challenge. Use positive peer pressure and hang out with friends who support your decision to wait, and who have made the same decision.

22. What if my boyfriend wants to end our relationship because of my decision?

A person who is willing to end a relationship just because you won't have sex with them probably never loved you in the first place. You have to stand up for what you believe, and remind him that if he really loves you, he would wait for you.

23. How can I keep my commitment?

It will help if you reflect on why you made the commitment to yourself. You have to decide if you want a stable, loving, dependable relationship or a temporary weak love, going from person to person and all the heartache that it causes. It also helps to surround yourself with positive people who will offer you the encouragement that you need.

24. How do I keep myself from giving into sexual urges?

You can keep yourself from giving into sexual urges by taking control of the environment that you are in and making lifestyle choices that support your decisions.

25. Can I be popular while I practice abstinence?

First, it is a myth that sexual activity makes you popular in a positive way. Your friends will respect you more, if you have the courage to stand by your values. You should find people who share your beliefs and interests instead of changing yourself to fit others.

26. Is it okay to think about sex?

It is natural to think about sex. However, thinking about sex is the first step in the process of physical sexual arousal. This can sabotage your decision to remain abstinent.

27. What if no one else in my family is practicing abstinence?

You might be in a situation where you have older sisters or brothers who have not made the decision to practice abstinence, but you don't have to follow in their footsteps. You have to make your own decisions, just as they have to make theirs.

28. What if I have sex after I have made my commitment?

Stop having sex and start over again, but don't make it a habit of breaking your commitment with yourself and God.

29. Should I look down on someone else who is not practicing abstinence?

No, you don't have the right to look down on anyone. Everyone has a choice. It is left up to each individual to decide what she wants to do.

30. What are the benefits of remaining abstinent?

First and foremost, you are pleasing God. You don't have to worry about ruining your reputation and your relationships. You don't have to be fearful of contracting a sexually transmitted disease or becoming a parent before you are ready.

Some Final Thoughts

I hope that you have enjoyed reading this book, and I am confident that you will make the right choice and not have sex until marriage. I want to encourage you to be strong, and my prayer is that you will remain empowered.

I invite you to visit my website at www.whyiwaited.com to share how this book has been a blessing to you. Your personal story will be a testament of God's sustaining power. I will continue to keep you in my prayers.

God Bless,

Angela R. Camon